Vroom, vroom, Baboon!

Russell Punter

Illustrated by David Semple

Baboon's a racing driver.
Her car goes super fast.

Her crew fine tunes the engine.

Another driver hides nearby –
Baboon's great rival, Cheetah.

That night, he creeps up to her car
and gives a sneaky grin.

The next day, all the cars get set.
Their engines rev...

vroom!

vroom!

Above the track, five lights go out.
The race has started.

ZOOM!

With twenty laps ahead of them,
Baboon soon takes the lead.

They hurtle around
the curving turns.

The laps go flying by.

Baboon keeps out of Cheetah's reach.

Cheetah calls his pit-stop squad.
"We need Plan B!" he squeals.

She steers around the obstacles, but one tack hits her tank.

Gluey fuel comes oozing out
all thanks to Cheetah's prank.

Baboon's fast car is slowing down.

Baboon just makes the winning flag.

The others
whoosh past fast.

She takes her prize,
while Cheetah sighs.

Starting to read

Even before children start to recognize words, they can learn about the pleasures of reading. Encouraging a love of stories and a joy in language is the best place to start.

About phonics

When children learn to read in school, they are often taught to recognize words through phonics. This teaches them to identify the sounds of letters that are then put together to make words. An important first step is for children to hear rhymes, which help them to listen out for the sounds in words.

You can find out more about phonics on the Usborne website at **usborne.com/Phonics**

Phonics Readers

These rhyming books provide the perfect combination of fun and phonics. They are lively and entertaining with great storylines and quirky illustrations. They have the added bonus of focusing on certain sounds so in this story your child will soon identify the *oo* sound, as in **vroom** and **Baboon.** Look out, too, for rhymes such as **squeals** – **wheels** and **fast** – **last.**

Reading with your child

If your child is reading a story to you, don't rush to correct mistakes, but be ready to prompt or guide if needed. Above all, give plenty of praise and encouragement.

Edited by Lesley Sims
Designed by Hope Reynolds

Reading consultants: Alison Kelly and Anne Washtell

First published in 2024 by Usborne Publishing Limited, 83-85 Saffron Hill, London EC1N 8RT, United Kingdom. usborne.com Copyright © 2024 Usborne Publishing Limited. The name Usborne and the Balloon logo are registered trade marks of Usborne Publishing Limited. UE.